Text by Ceece Kelley
Illustrations by Marina Halak
This book was edited by Tamara Rittershaus and designed by Elizabeth Jayasekera.
The production was supervised by Ceece Kelley.

ISBN 978-1-953859-60-0

Library of Congress Control Number: 2022941406

This is a work of fiction. Names, characters, places and incidents either are the product of the author's imagination or are used fictitiously. Any resemblance to actual persons, living or dead, events or locales is entirely coincidental.

The publisher is not responsible for websites (or their content) that are not owned by the publisher.

First edition 2023. Printed and bound in China.

Distributed by Lerner Publishing Group, Inc.
241 First Avenue North
Minneapolis, MN 55401 U.S.A

For reading levels and more information, look for this title on www.lernerbooks.com

Soaring Kite Books, LLC
Washington, D.C.
United States of America
www.soaringkitebooks.com

To every family who has loved and lost, including my own.
I wish you healing, comfort, and joy for what lies ahead. —CK

To my family. —MH

Ceece Kelley

Marina Halak

A Book for Rainbow Babies

Rainbow Letters

 Soaring Kite Books

In a dreamy kingdom tucked away
past cotton candy skies,
there's a land of little helpers,
rosy-cheeked and sparkly-eyed.

Each and every one of us
looks forward to the day
when we hear the joyous news—
a rainbow sibling's on the way!

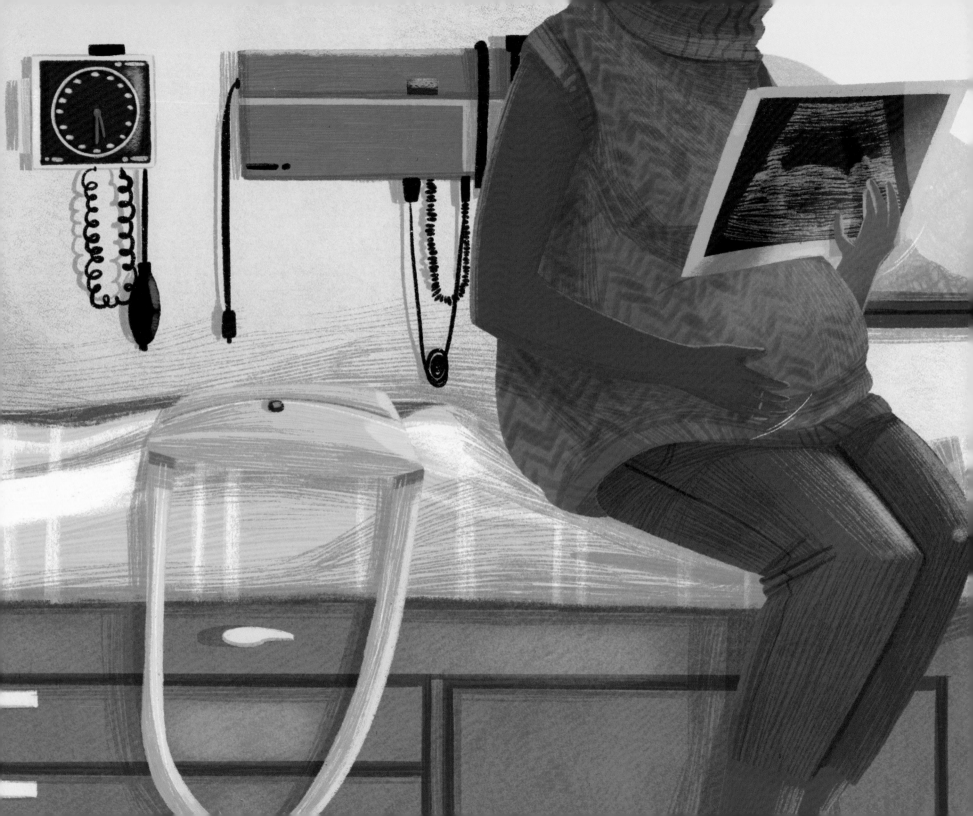

You are a rainbow baby:
the calm after the storm,
the sun after cloudy days,
one less reason to mourn.

And once we heard you were on the way,
there wasn't a moment to lose.
We wrote our Rainbow Letters
and made your blanket in soft hues.

A Rainbow Letter is a message
from a sibling you never knew,
to share our joy and gladness
and soothe our parents too.

Then we sewed it onto your blanket,
the one that's pink and blue.
We warmed it up with hugs and love,
and sibling kisses too.

You were wrapped up in this blanket
when you stepped into the world,
and with one look at little you,
our parents' hearts unfurled.

And now it is your time to shine.
You'll bring us hope and love.
And every milestone you achieve,
we'll cheer you on from above.

You'll always have a sibling
who really loves you so.
We know that you'll remember us
as you learn and grow.

Precious
Child

We celebrate your life
as ours is remembered too,
and know that every single day,
we'll be watching over you.

My *Rainbow Letter* said:

Place your rainbow baby's ultrasound picture here:

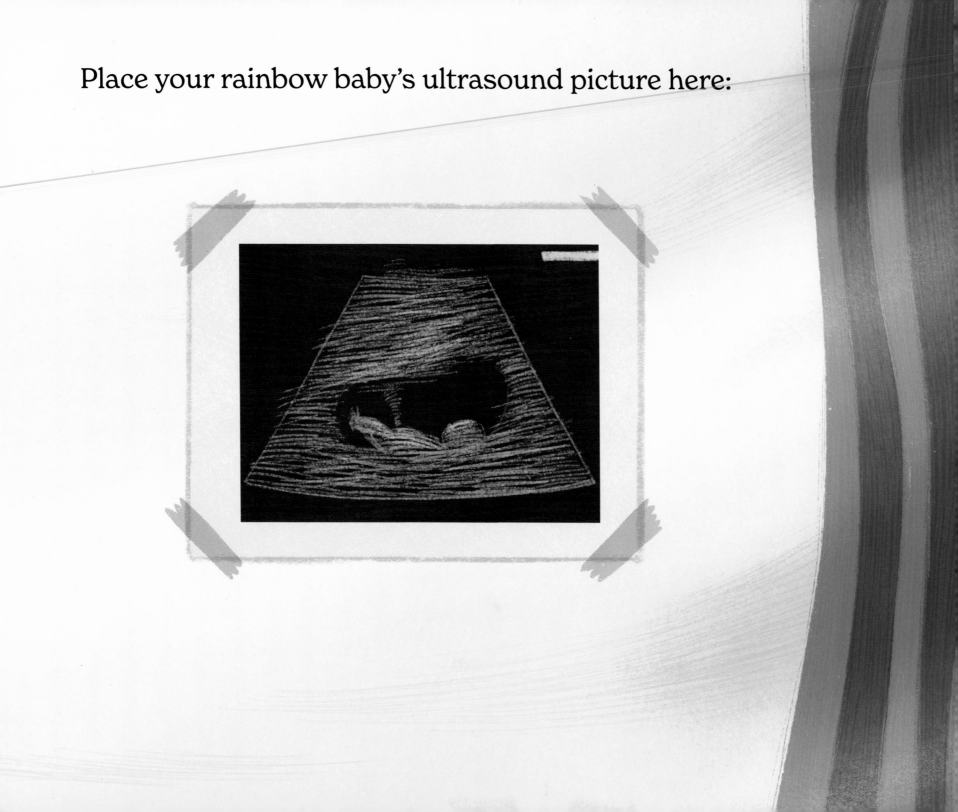

A Message from Dr. Cassidy Freitas

Dear Parents,

If you're reading this, I imagine you've experienced the heartbreak of losing a child during pregnancy, birth, or postpartum. Pregnancy loss was the most isolating experience of grief I've ever walked through. I want to take this opportunity to share with you a few things I wish I could go back and tell myself in my darkest hours.

1) You are not alone. Pregnancy and child loss touches many, and support is out there. Sometimes we have to take the meaningful risk of opening up to those we trust to receive the support we so need.

2) Pregnancy and child loss can impact each of us in different ways. My partner and I experienced the loss very differently, and couples therapy supported us in feeling connected again.

3) Sometimes people will say things that aren't helpful. "Everything happens for a reason" was a common one, and while I have processed the loss and have made meaning of the experience for myself, I didn't want the reason for this loss—I wanted that child in my arms. It's important to set boundaries where you need them.

4) Pregnancy and child loss can be traumatic. You deserve support to process and heal. Postpartum Support International has resources for you too.

Tips for sharing *Rainbow Letters* and addressing this loss with your child:

Understand that as children get older, the meaning of the book will grow and change, but the routine of connecting with you through the cadence of the book will be supportive and comforting from the start.

Choose an annual ritual that feels meaningful to you and include your children now and as they grow. Ideas could include: planting a memorial tree that can be visited, lighting a candle, praying, or sharing a special meal.

Explore ways to incorporate meaningful symbols into your life with your child. For example: if a rainbow becomes a symbol, you can incorporate symbolic décor in your home or practice pausing and appreciating the meaning of a rainbow with your child when you witness one. Butterflies became a symbol for us, and we now have a tradition of honoring the child we lost by visiting a butterfly garden with our children every spring.

If your child asks questions or makes comments about the loss, they are old enough to receive answers and witness the story of the sibling they didn't get to meet. Talk slowly, make eye contact, and check in with their feelings. This could be a great opportunity to reshare their Rainbow Letter with them too.

Jewelry can also have special meaning. I have a rainbow necklace I wear every day, and it's a constant reminder of the child I carry in my heart and has prompted meaningful conversations with my children as well.

If this book has found its way to you, you don't need to walk through this alone. I hope you offer yourself the same loving care that you give so intentionally to your rainbow baby.

Dr. Cassidy Freitas, Licensed Marriage and Family Therapist
Host of the Holding Space Podcast for parents
www.drcassidymft.com
Let's also connect on Instagram @drcassidy